Dr. K-2

BEECHWOOD BUNNY TALES

VIOLETTE'S
Daring
Adventure

For a free color catalog describing Gareth Stevens' list of
high-quality books, call 1-800-341-3569 (USA)
or 1-800-461-9120 (Canada).

Beechwood Bunny Tales
Dandelion's Vanishing Vegetable Garden
Mistletoe and the Baobab Tree
Periwinkle at the Full Moon Ball
Poppy's Dance
Aunt Zinnia and the Ogre
Violette's Daring Adventure
Family Moving Day

Library of Congress Cataloging-in-Publication Data

Huriet, Geneviève.
　　[Défi de Pirouette Passiflore. English]
　　Violette's daring adventure / written by Geneviève Huriet;
illustrated by Loïc Jouannigot. — North American ed., U.S. ed.
　　　p. cm. — (Beechwood bunny tales)
　　Summary: Two bunnies, Violette Bellflower and her brother
Periwinkle, learn that Papa is right: the pond is a dangerous place to play.
　　ISBN 0-8368-0912-2
　　[1. Rabbits—Fiction. 2. Foxes—Fiction.] 3. Brothers and
sisters—Fiction.] I. Jouannigot, Loïc, ill. II. Title. III. Series:
Huriet, Geneviève. Beechwood bunny tales.
PZ7.H95657Vi　1992　　[E]—dc20　　　　92-30430

North American edition first published in 1992 by
Gareth Stevens Publishing
1555 North RiverCenter Drive, Suite 201
Milwaukee, Wisconsin 53212, USA

English text by Amy Bauman

Printed in the United States of America

1 2 3 4 5 6 7 8 9 97 96 95 94 93 92

BEECHWOOD BUNNY TALES

VIOLETTE'S
Daring
Adventure

written by GENEVIÈVE HURIET
illustrated by LOÏC JOUANNIGOT

Gareth Stevens Publishing
MILWAUKEE

It was another bright autumn afternoon in Beechwood Grove. Periwinkle and Violette Bellflower, tempted by the warm sunshine and the sound of crunching leaves, went outside to play. Only Aunt Zinnia's fresh apple pie kept Mistletoe, Poppy, and Dandelion from going, too.

"Let's walk down to the pond," Violette suggested to her brother, and the two bunnies set off at a brisk pace.

The Bellflower children thought the pond was a great place to play. Not everyone agreed.

"The pond is too far from home," Papa often said. "It could be dangerous."

But Violette was not thinking of her father's warning as she picked up smooth, flat stones from along the pond's edge. She and Periwinkle took turns skipping the stones across the water. "Ooh, Periwinkle! Mine skipped three times!"

"Good shot!" came a strange voice.

The startled bunnies looked up to see a boy seated on the opposite bank. He had a cap pulled nearly over his eyes, and a bulky muffler hid the rest of his face.

"Who are you?" Periwinkle called bravely from behind his sister.

"Jimmy Renard," the boy answered. "Come play with me."

As the bunnies watched, the boy pulled a harmonica from his pocket. The notes floated gently across the pond.

"That's pretty!" they called when he had finished his song.

"Play another!"

"My hands are too cold. Let's go to my house, and then I'll play another," he called, adding, "My mother's baking chocolate chip cookies. . . ."

"Cookies?" the bunnies repeated. They looked at each other for a moment but could not resist. "Let's go!"

Jimmy Renard set off without waiting for the bunnies.

"Wait for us!" Periwinkle cried, ready to hop after him.

"Where is your house?" Violette asked. She kept a firm grip on Periwinkle's hand.

The boy pointed toward a tangle of beech trees ahead of them. As he did, his muffler slipped down his nose a bit before he could catch it. Violette's quick eyes spotted his pointed, brown snout.

"Oh, no!" Violette whispered to herself. Jimmy Renard was a . . . a FOX!

"Periwinkle!" Violette hissed, trying to catch her brother's attention.

Periwinkle didn't hear her. A few steps ahead, he danced and pranced to a song he'd just made up. The words went something like: "Cookies! We're going to have cookies!" He sang them over and over to himself.

Suddenly, Violette began humming. Loudly, she hummed the tune to their grandfather's favorite song: "Alert, alert, little bunnies! The enemy is near!"

Periwinkle heard her, and he stopped dancing in the middle of a beautiful twirl.

"Jimmy Renard is a real fox!" she quickly whispered.

"Quick!" Periwinkle cried. "Let's run away while his back is turned!"

"I have a better idea," Violette said. "We'll trick him. We'll follow him until we reach the rocks. Then, just when he thinks he has trapped us . . . ZIP! . . . we'll disappear into the Big Passage."

15

The Big Passage was a secret tunnel. It ran from one end of Beechwood Grove to the other and had many entrances. The rabbits hid in the tunnel whenever danger threatened. One of its entrances was just ahead.

"Are you coming?" Jimmy called back impatiently.

Hand in hand, the bunnies trooped after him.

"Just ten more steps, then spin to the right," Violette whispered. Her heart beat excitedly. She imagined how the other bunnies would "ooh" and "aah" when they heard how she and Periwinkle had outfoxed the fox.

Suddenly, another fox leaped out at the bunnies.

"Catch them, Arthur!" Jimmy Renard cried, throwing off his disguise.

The two bunnies darted away with the foxes close behind them. Through the heather and under the ferns they ran, zigzagging this way and that.

But the foxes were good hunters. With a quick turn, Arthur cornered poor, tired Periwinkle.

"We're too quick for you, little bunny," Arthur shouted, grabbing hold of Periwinkle. The two foxes chuckled nastily. From behind the bushes, Violette watched them drag her brother away.

"Oh, this is all my fault," she cried softly. "I should never have tried to be so clever." Not knowing what else to do, she followed the foxes to their dark, dingy burrow.

When the foxes had gone inside, Violette crept to the door.
"You hold him while I tie him up," Jimmy was saying to
Arthur. "What a wonderful dinner we'll have tonight!"

"Dinner!" Violette gulped. No one was going to make a
dinner of her brother — not if she could help it. As Jimmy
turned away, she burst quickly through the door. With one
kick from her powerful back feet, she sent Arthur tumbling to
the ground.

Like lightning, Violette struck and was gone — her brother
in tow. Without looking back, the bunnies shot out of the
house and down the path. In another moment, angry fox
screams filled the air, and fox footsteps fell heavily behind them.

"Run this way, Periwinkle," Violette panted. "Run for the
Big Passage."

Through the bushes and into the tunnel the bunnies ran. But the foxes did not give up.

"After them!" Jimmy shrieked.

Suddenly, dirt and pebbles showered down in front of the foxes. Sputtering dirt, they looked angrily at the sealed-off tunnel. Violette and Periwinkle had outfoxed them after all.

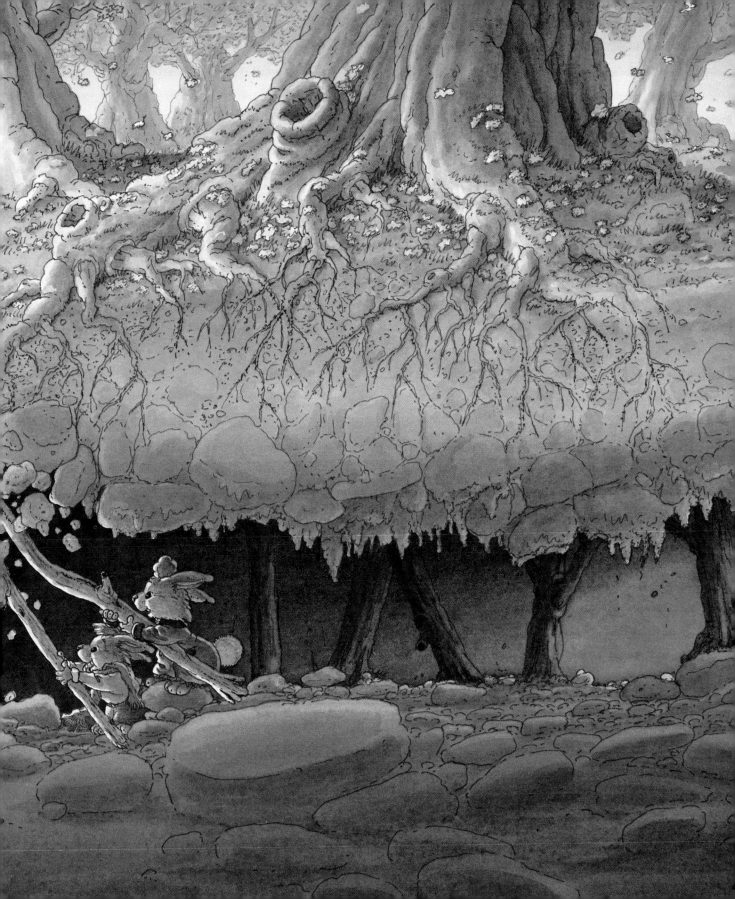

Violette and Periwinkle ran until they reached home.

"Where have you been?" Papa Bramble asked excitedly, meeting his dirty, breathless children on the steps.

"Oh, Papa!" Violette exclaimed. "Two foxes near the pond tried to trap us in the Big Passage, but we collapsed the tunnel, and they couldn't find us. Wasn't that brave, Papa?"

"It sounds very brave . . . but very dangerous," Papa Bramble said. He tried to sound stern, but inside he felt very proud of his children.

That night at dinner, Mistletoe, Poppy, and Dandelion begged for details of the adventure. But Violette and Periwinkle were too tired to talk — or even to eat. Well before dessert, Papa and Aunt Zinnia carried them off to bed.

But after such fearful adventures, the bunnies did not sleep well. Both tossed and turned with terrible nightmares.

"Oh, no! The foxes!" Violette cried out. "They've captured Periwinkle!"

"Let go! Let go!" Periwinkle moaned.

"It's only a bad dream," Papa soothed, tucking his children in once more.

"I will never try to be more clever than the fox again," Violette mumbled, still half asleep.

"It seems the children haven't told me the entire story," Papa murmured to himself. Sighing, he returned to bed.